MW00985341

This book belongs to

_____

DONALD DUCK DIRECTS

Disney's

READ and GROW LIBRARY

Published by Advance Publishers
Winter Park, Florida

Written by Marc Gave   Edited by Bonnie Brook
Penciled by Peter J. Alvarado   Painted by William Dely
Designed by Design Five
Cover art by Peter Emslie
Cover design by Irene Yap

ISBN: 1-885222-89-0
10 9 8 7 6 5 4 3 2 1

"Donald!" yelled Scrooge McDuck. "Get in here!"

Donald raced into Scrooge's office. "Yes sir," said Donald. "I'm sorry about anything I may have done wrong—"

"Quiet!" said Scrooge. "I've just had a great idea! I want a movie made about my life!"

"I'll do it, Uncle Scrooge," said Donald excitedly. "I've always wanted to make a movie."

"Make sure you include everything," said Scrooge. "I want you to show the world who the real Scrooge McDuck is."

"You've got it, boss!" said Donald.

Donald raced down the hallway. "Oh, boy! Oh, boy!" he said.

Then he had a thought. A few minutes later he returned to Scrooge's office with Mickey and Goofy.

"Now what?" said Scrooge.

"Can Mickey and Goofy help?" asked Donald.

"Fine," said Scrooge. "Now just leave me alone and get to work."

"We'll do a good job, Mr. McDuck," said Mickey.

"Gawrsh, no!" said Goofy. "We'll do a *great* job."

Donald led Mickey and Goofy to one of Scrooge's buildings on the outskirts of Duckburg. "Well, here it is, guys," he said, "the home of our very own film company."

"Gawrsh," said Goofy, looking around. "It just looks like an empty building to me."

"Wait until we get all our things in," said Donald.

The next day Donald sat in his newly furnished office.

"Not bad, eh, boys?" said Donald, kicking his feet up on his desk and pointing around the office. "We've got a telephone, a fax machine, a photocopier, a computer system, a camera and film, lights, and a sound system. And that's not all. In some of the other rooms we also have an editing machine and equipment for making videos of the film."

"Gawrsh," said Goofy. "Could you slow down so my brain can catch up?"

"Well," said Donald, "this is a fax machine. It's almost like a telephone, but instead of sending your voice the way a telephone does, it prints written words and pictures on paper."

Goofy was confused. "Can this fax machine help us make our movie?"

"Not exactly," said Donald. "But you know how Uncle Scrooge hates answering the phone when he's counting his money. If we have questions, I can just send him a fax."

"What about this computer?" asked Goofy. "Can it help us make our movie?"

"It sure can," Donald answered. "I'll use it to type a script."

"A what?" Goofy asked.

"A script is like a story. It tells what's going to happen in the movie," said Mickey.

"Oops," said Goofy. "I think I just turned this machine on."

"That's a photocopier," Mickey said with a laugh as he pulled a picture of Goofy's hand from the machine. "It's *usually* used to make copies of pieces of paper—like Donald's script."

"Boy, all these things run on electricity," said Goofy, catching on. "What's next?"

Donald took them into another room that had a computer, too. But this computer was different—it had more add-ons, buttons and switches than the other.

"What can this computer do?" exclaimed Goofy. "Send us into outer space? A-hyuck!"

"This is for editing our film," said Donald. "We'll use it to cut out parts we don't like and put together the parts of the film we want to use in our movie."

"Do you know how to use this thing?" asked Mickey.

"Piece of cake!" said Donald. But Mickey wasn't so sure.

"Now, here's where we'll do some of our filming," said Donald.

"Huh?" said Goofy.

"We'll use the movie camera to make moving pictures of the actors," Mickey explained.

"How do we do that?" asked Goofy.

"You can shine the lights, and Mickey can record the sounds," Donald answered. "Of course, I'll direct."

"Who's going to run the camera?" asked Mickey.

"Nothin' to it!" Donald replied boldly. "I'll direct *and* run the camera."

Donald led his pals into yet another room. It was also filled with lots of equipment.

"In this room," Donald began, "we copy the film onto videotape. We can sell videotapes after the movie is finished showing in theaters."

But Goofy wasn't even listening anymore. He had pushed a tape into the VCR and was laughing at the movie that was playing on the television.

Donald thought maybe it was a good time to pay a visit to Uncle Scrooge and let him know how he was doing.

"What!" Scrooge yelled when he saw all the bills.

"Uh, Uncle Scrooge," Donald began. "We needed office furniture and equipment, a camera and film, and . . ."

"A videotape machine?" Scrooge shouted.

"That's so we can sell tapes and make a lot of money," said Donald.

"Oh!" said Scrooge happily. "Good thinking, Donald!".

"By the way," said Scrooge, "when *are* you going to start shooting the film? I'm sending out these invitations to opening night at the Duckburg Cinema."

Donald looked at the date—it was only one week away!

"Uh, I was just going to do that right now!" said Donald, as he ran out of Scrooge's office.

"Aw, phooey!" said Donald when he returned to his office. "How am I supposed to finish a whole movie in a week? We don't have a script. Nobody's even shown me how to use the camera."

"Gawrsh, Donald," said Goofy. "What are we gonna do?"

"Cheer up, guys," said Mickey. "Since we don't have much time, why don't we just make *A Day in the Life of Scrooge McDuck*? Then we'll have the rest of the week to put the film together."

"Great idea!" shouted Donald.

The three pals sat up all night figuring out how to use the movie camera, the sound machine, and the lights.

The next day, they showed up at Scrooge's house at dawn. They followed him to his factories, his stores, his office, and even down to his vault. They filmed Scrooge at each location.

By the end of the day, Donald was sure he had enough film to make a movie.

"Now what?" said Goofy.

Donald looked at the film. Then he looked at Mickey.

"Uh—Mickey?" asked Donald. "Do you know what we are supposed to do next?"

"With my video camera, I just take the tape out, pop it into my VCR, and watch," said Goofy.

"I think this is different," said Mickey. "You need to get the film processed first."

"Wak!" said Donald. "Where?! How?!"

Luckily, they found a lab that promised to have the film back in a jiffy.

"Gawrsh, making a film was fun," said Goofy, when they picked it up from the lab.

"I don't think we're done yet," said Mickey. "We still have to edit the film."

It was a hard job to decide what parts to keep in and what parts to take out. Every scene was somehow about money: Scrooge dusting stacks of twenty-dollar bills; Scrooge draining a fishpond to collect the pennies; Scrooge selling his old clothes.

GREAT DEAL!

CHEAP!

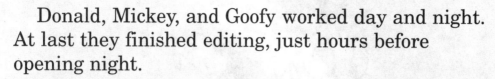

Donald, Mickey, and Goofy worked day and night. At last they finished editing, just hours before opening night.

Everyone who was anyone came to the Duckburg Cinema, dressed in fine clothes. TV cameras rolled, and searchlights lit up the sky. It was some event!

After everyone was seated, the lights went out. *All* the lights went out. It was pitch black in the theater.

"Who turned out the lights?" shouted Goofy.

"Power failure!" Donald shouted.

"Don't panic!" yelled Mickey.

Donald suddenly felt a tug at his sleeve.

Then Uncle Scrooge's familiar voice whispered, "I got a sneak preview of the film, and I couldn't let you show it. I looked like a mean, old, money-grubbing miser."

Donald sighed. All that work for nothing.

The next morning Scrooge called Donald to his office.

"I was thinking," Scrooge began. "I'd like to start on a new movie right away. But this time, instead of you following me around with that camera, I want a made-up story, an action-adventure tale. I want one of those action-movie actors to play the part of me. But I don't want to pay all that money. So I decided on the perfect duck to star in the film—you!"

"Me?" said a surprised Donald. "Well, why not?"